The New Atlantis

Sir Francis Bacon

INTRODUCTORY NOTE

Bacon's literary executor, Dr. Rowley, published *The New Atlantis* in 1627, the year after the author's death. It seems to have been written about 1623, during that period of literary activity which followed Bacon's political fall. None of Bacon's writings gives in short apace so vivid a picture of his tastes and aspirations as this fragment of the plan of an ideal commonwealth. The generosity and enlightenment, the dignity and splendor, the piety and public spirit, of the inhabitants of Bensalem represent the ideal qualities which Bacon the statesman desired rather than hoped to see characteristic of his own country; and in Solomon's House we have Bacon the scientist indulging without restriction his prophetic vision of the future of human knowledge. No reader acquainted in any degree with the processes and results of modern scientific inquiry can fail to be struck by the numerous approximations made by Bacon's imagination to the actual achievements of modern times. The plan and organization of his great college lay down the main lines of the modern research university; and both in pure and applied science he anticipates a strikingly large number of recent inventions and discoveries. In still another way is *The New Atlantis* typical of Bacon's attitude. In spite of the enthusiastic and broad-minded schemes he laid down for the pursuit of truth, Bacon always had an eye to utility. The advancement of science which he sought was conceived by him as a means to a practical end the increase of man's control over nature, and the comfort and convenience of humanity. For pure metaphysics, or any form of abstract thinking that yielded no "fruit," he had little interest; and this leaning to the useful is shown in the practical applications of the discoveries made by the scholars of Solomon's House. Nor does the interest of the work stop here. It contains much, both in its political and in its scientific ideals, that we have as yet by no means achieved, but which contain valuable elements of suggestion and stimulus for the future.

The New Atlantis

We sailed from Peru, (where we had continued for the space of one whole year) for China and Japan, by the South Sea; taking with us victuals for twelve months; and had good winds from the east, though soft and weak, for five months space, and more. But the wind came about, and settled in the west for many days, so as we could make little or no way, and were sometime in purpose to turn back. But then again there arose strong and great winds from the south, with a point east, which carried us up (for all that we could do) towards the north; by which time our victuals failed us, though we had made good spare of them. So that finding ourselves, in the midst of the greatest wilderness of waters in the world, without victuals, we gave ourselves for lost men and prepared for death. Yet we did lift up our hearts and voices to God above, who showeth his wonders in the deep, beseeching him of his mercy, that as in the beginning he discovered the face of the deep, and brought forth dry land, so he would not discover land to us, that we might not perish.

And it came to pass that the next day about evening we saw within a kenning before us, towards the north, as it were thick clouds, which did put us in some hope of land; knowing how that part of the South Sea was utterly unknown; and might have islands, or continents, that hitherto were not come to light. Wherefore we bent our course thither, where we saw the appearance of land, all that night; and in the dawning of the next day, we might plainly discern that it was a land; flat to our sight, and full of boscage; which made it show the more dark. And after an hour and a half's sailing, we entered into a good haven, being the port of a fair city; not great indeed, but well built, and that gave a pleasant view from the sea: and we thinking every minute long, till we were on land, came close to the shore, and offered to land. But straightways we saw divers of the people, with *bastons* in their hands (as it were) forbidding us to land; yet without any cries of fierceness, but only as warning us off, by signs that they made. Whereupon being not a little discomforted, we were advising with ourselves, what we should do.

During which time, there made forth to us a small boat, with about eight persons in it; whereof one of them had in his hand a tipstaff of a yellow cane, tipped at both ends with blue, who came aboard our ship, without any show of distrust at all. And when he saw one of our number, present himself somewhat before the rest, he drew forth a little scroll of parchment (somewhat yellower than our parchment, and shining like the leaves of writing tables, but otherwise soft and flexible,) and delivered it to our foremost man. In which scroll were written in ancient Hebrew, and in ancient Greek, and in good Latin of the school, and in Spanish, these words:

Land ye not, none of you; and provide to be gone from this coast, within sixteen days, except you have further time given you. Meanwhile, if you want fresh water or victuals, or help for your sick, or that your ship needeth repairs, write down your wants, and you shall have that, which belongeth to mercy.

This scroll was signed with a stamp of cherubim: wings, not spread, but hanging downwards; and by them a cross. This being delivered, the officer returned, and left only a servant with us to receive our answer.

Consulting hereupon amongst ourselves, we were much perplexed. The denial of landing and hasty warning us away troubled us much; on the other side, to find that the people had languages, and were so full of humanity, did comfort us not a little. And above all, the sign of the cross to that instrument was to us a great rejoicing, and as it were a certain presage of good. Our answer was in the Spanish tongue; that for our ship, it was well; for we had rather met with calms and contrary winds than any tempests. For our sick, they were many, and in very ill case; so that if they were not permitted to land, they ran danger of their lives. Our other wants we set down in particular; adding, That we had some little store of merchandise, which if it pleased them to deal for, it might supply our wants, without being chargeable unto them. We offered some reward in *pistolets* unto the servant, and a piece of crimson velvet to be presented to the officer; but the servant took them not, nor would scarce look upon them; and so left us, and went back in another little boat, which was sent for him.

About three hours after we had dispatched our answer, there came towards us a person (as it seemed) of place. He had on him a gown with wide sleeves, of a kind of water chamolet, of an excellent azure colour, fair more glossy than ours; his under apparel was green; and so was his hat, being in the form of a turban, daintily made, and not so huge as the Turkish turbans; and the locks of his hair came down below the brims of it. A reverend man was he to behold. He came in a boat, gilt in some part of it, with four persons more only in that boat; and was followed by another boat, wherein were some twenty. When he was come within a flightshot of our ship, signs were made to us, that we should send forth some to meet him upon the water; which we presently did in our ship-boat, sending the principal man amongst us save one, and four of our number with him.

When we were come within six yards of their boat, they called to us to stay, and not to approach farther; which we did. And thereupon the man, whom I before described, stood up, and with a loud voice, in Spanish, asked, "Are ye Christians?" We answered, "We were;" fearing the less, because of the cross we had seen in the subscription. At which answer the said person lifted up his right hand towards Heaven, and drew it softly to his mouth (which is the gesture they use, when they thank God;) and then said : "If ye will swear (all of you) by the merits of the Saviour, that ye are no pirates, nor have shed blood, lawfully, nor unlawfully within forty days past, you may have licence to come on land." We said, "We were all ready to take that oath." Whereupon one of those that were with him, being (as it seemed) a notary, made an entry of this act. Which done, another of the attendants of the great person which was with him in the same boat, after his Lord had spoken a little to him, said aloud: "My Lord would have you know, that it is not of pride, or greatness, that he cometh not aboard your ship; but for that in your answer you declare that you have many sick amongst you, he was warned by the Conservator of Health of the city that he should keep a distance." We bowed ourselves towards him, and answered, "We were his humble servants; and accounted for great honour, and singular humanity towards us, that which was already done; but hoped well, that the nature of the sickness of our men was not infectious." So he returned; and a while after came the Notary to us aboard our ship; holding in his hand a fruit of that country, like an orange, but of colour between orange-tawney and scarlet; which cast a most excellent odour. He used it (as it seemeth) for a preservative against infection. He gave us our oath; "By the name of Jesus, and his merits:" and after told us, that the next day, by six of the Clock, in the Morning, we should be sent to, and brought to the Strangers' House, (so he called it,) where we should be accommodated of things, both for our whole, and for our sick. So he left us; and when we offered him some *pistolets*, he smiling said, "He must not be twice paid for one labour:" meaning (as I take it) that he had salary sufficient of the State for his service. For (as I after learned) they call an officer that taketh rewards, "twice paid."

The next morning early, there came to us the same officer that came to us at first with his cane, and told us, He came to conduct us to the Strangers' House; and that he had prevented the hour, because we might have the whole day before us, for our business. "For," said he, "if you will follow my advice, there shall first go with me some few of you, and see the place, and how it may be made convenient for you; and then you may send for your sick, and the rest of your number, which ye will bring on land." We thanked him, and said, "That this care, which he took of desolate strangers, God would reward." And so six of us went on land with him: and when we were on land, he went before us, and turned to us, and said, "He was but our servant, and our guide." He led us through three fair streets; and all the way we went, there were gathered some people on both sides, standing in a row; but in so civil a fashion, as if it had been, not to wonder at us, but to welcome us: and divers of them, as we passed by them, put their arms a little abroad; which is their gesture, when they did bid any welcome.

The Strangers' House is a fair and spacious house, built of brick, of somewhat a bluer colour than our brick; and with handsome windows, some of glass, some of a kind of cambric oiled. He brought us first into a fair parlour above stairs, and then asked us, "What number of persons we were? And how many sick?" We answered, "We were in all, (sick and whole,) one and fifty persons, whereof our sick were seventeen." He desired us to have patience a little, and to stay till he came back to us; which was about an hour after; and then he led us to see the chambers which were provided for us, being in number nineteen: they having cast it (as it seemeth) that four of those chambers, which were better than the rest, might receive four of the principal men of our company; and lodge them alone by themselves; and the other fifteen chambers were to lodge us two and two together. The chambers were handsome and cheerful chambers, and furnished civilly." Then he led us to a long gallery, like a *dorture*, where he showed us all along the one side (for the other side was but wall and window), seventeen cells, very neat ones, having partitions of cedar wood. Which gallery and cells, being in all forty, many more than we needed, were instituted as an infirmary for sick persons. And he told us withal, that as any of our sick waxed well, he might be removed from his cell, to a chamber; for which purpose there were set forth ten spare chambers, besides the number we spake of before. This done, he brought us back to the parlour, and lifting up his cane a little, (as they do when they give any charge or command) said to us, "Ye are to know, that the custom of the land requireth, that after this day and to-morrow, (which we give you for removing of your people from your ship,) you are to keep within doors for three days. But let it not trouble you, nor do not think yourselves restrained, but rather left to your rest and ease. You shall want nothing, and there are six of our people appointed to attend you, for any business you may have abroad." We gave him thanks, with all affection and respect, and said, "God surely is manifested in this land." We offered him also twenty *pistolets*; but he smiled, and only said; "What? twice paid!" And so he left us.

Soon after our dinner was served in; which was right good viands, both for bread and treat: better than any collegiate diet, that I have known in Europe. We had also drink of three sorts, all wholesome and good; wine of the grape; a drink of grain, such as is with us our ale, but more clear: And a kind of cider made of a fruit of that country; a wonderful pleasing and refreshing drink. Besides, there were brought in to us, great store of those scarlet oranges, for our sick; which (they said) were an assured remedy for sickness taken at sea. There was given us also, a box of small gray, or whitish pills, which they wished our sick should take, one of the pills, every night before sleep; which (they said) would hasten their recovery.

The next day, after that our trouble of carriage and removing of our men and goods out of our ship, was somewhat settled and quiet, I thought good to call our company together; and when they were assembled, said unto them:

"My dear friends, let us know ourselves, and how it standeth with us. We are men cast on land, as Jonas was, out of the whale's belly, when we were as buried in the deep: and now we are on land, we are but between death and life; for we are beyond, both the old world, and the new; and whether ever we shall see Europe, God only knoweth. It is a kind of miracle bath brought us hither: and it must be little less, that shall bring us hence. Therefore in regard of our deliverance past, and our danger present, and to come, let us look up to God, and every man reform his own ways. Besides we are come here amongst a Christian people, full of piety and humanity: let us not bring that confusion of face upon ourselves, as to show our vices, or unworthiness before them. Yet there is more. For they have by commandment, (though in form of courtesy) cloistered us within these wall, for three days: who knoweth, whether it be not, to take some taste of our manners and conditions? And if they find them bad, to banish us straightways; if good, to give us further time. For these men that they have given us for attendance, may withal have an eye upon us. Therefore for God's love, and as we love the weal of our souls and bodies, let us so behave ourselves, as we may be at peace with God, and may find grace in the eyes of this people."

Our company with one voice thanked me for my good admonition, and promised me to live soberly and civilly, and without giving any the least occasion of offence. So we spent our three days joyfully, and without care, in expectation what would be done with us, when they were expired. During which time, we had every hour joy of the amendment of our sick; who thought themselves cast into some divine pool of healing; they mended so kindly, and so fast.

The morrow after our three days were past, there came to us a new man, that we had not seen before, clothed in blue as the former was, save that his turban was white, with a small red cross on the top. He had also a tippet of fine linen. At his coming in, he did bend to us a little, and put his arms abroad. We of our parts saluted him in a very lowly and submissive manner; as looking that from him, we should receive sentence of life, or death: he desired to speak with some few of us: whereupon six of us only staid, and the rest avoided the room. He said, "I am by office governor of this House of Strangers, and by vocation I am a Christian priest: and therefore am come to you to offer you my service, both as strangers and chiefly as Christians. Some things I may tell you, which I think you will not be unwilling to hear. The State hath given you license to stay on land, for the space of six weeks; and let it not trouble you, if your occasions ask further time, for the law in this point is not precise; and I do not doubt, but my self shall be able, to obtain for you such further time, as may be convenient. Ye shall also understand, that the Strangers' House is at this time rich, and much aforehand; for it hath laid up revenue these thirty-seven years; for so long it is since any stranger arrived in this part: and therefore take ye no care; the State will defray you all the time you stay; neither shall you stay one day the less for that. As for any merchandise ye have brought, ye shall be well used, and have your return, either in merchandise, or in gold and silver: for to us it is all one. And if you have any other request to make, hide it not. For ye shall find we will not make your countenance to fall by the answer ye shall receive. Only this I must tell you, that none of you must go above a karan," (that is with them a mile and an half) "from the walls of the city, without especial leave."

We answered, after we had looked awhile one upon another, admiring this gracious and parent-like usage; "That we could not tell what to say: for we wanted words to express our thanks; and his noble free offers left us nothing to ask. It seemed to us, that we had before us a picture of our salvation in Heaven; for we that were a while since in the jaws of death, were now brought into a place, where we found nothing but consolations. For the commandment laid upon us, we would not fail to obey it, though it was impossible but our hearts should be enflamed to tread further upon this happy and holy ground." We added, "That our tongues should first cleave to the roofs of our mouths, ere we should forget, either his reverend person, or this whole nation, in our prayers." We also most humbly besought him, to accept of us as his true servants; by as just a right as ever men on earth were bounden; laying and presenting, both our persons, and all we had, at his feet. He said; "He was a priest, and looked for a priest's reward; which was our brotherly love, and the good of our souls and bodies." So he went from us, not without tears of tenderness in his eyes; and left us also confused with joy and kindness, saying amongst ourselves; "That we were come into a land of angels, which did appear to us daily, and prevent us with comforts, which we thought not of, much less expected."

The next day about ten of the clock, the Governor came to us again, and after salutations, said familiarly; "That he was come to visit us;" and called for a chair, and sat him down: and we, being some ten of us, (the rest were of the meaner sort, or else gone abroad,) sat down with him, And when we were set, he began thus: " We of this island of Bensalem," (for so they call it in their language,) "have this; that by means of our solitary situation; and of the laws of secrecy, which we have for our travellers, and our rare admission of strangers; we know well most part of the habitable world, and are ourselves unknown. Therefore because he that knoweth least is fittest to ask questions, it is more reason, for the entertainment of the time, that ye ask me questions, than that I ask you."

We answered; "That we humbly thanked him that he would give us leave so to do: and that we conceived by the taste we had already, that there was no worldly thing on earth, more worthy to be known than the state of that happy land. But above all," (we said,) "since that we were met from the several ends of the world, and hoped assuredly that we should meet one day in the kingdom of Heaven, (for that we were both parts Christians,) we desired to know, (in respect that land was so remote, and so divided by vast and unknown seas, from the land where our Saviour walked on earth,) who was the apostle of that nation, and how it was converted to the faith?" It appeared in his face that he took great contentment in this our question: he said; "Ye knit my heart to you, by asking this question in the first place; for it sheweth that you first seek the kingdom of heaven; and I shall gladly, and briefly, satisfy your demand.

"About twenty years after the ascension of our Saviour, it came to pass, that there was seen by the people of Renfusa, (a city upon the eastern coast of our island,) within night, (the night was cloudy, and calm,) as it might be some mile into the sea, a great pillar of light; not sharp, but in form of a column, or cylinder, rising from the sea a great way up towards heaven; and on the top of it was seen a large cross of light, more bright and resplendent than the body of the pillar. Upon which so strange a spectacle, the people of the city gathered apace together upon the sands, to wonder; and so after put themselves into a number of small boats, to go nearer to this marvellous sight. But when the boats were come within (about) sixty yards of the pillar, they found themselves all bound, and could go no further; yet so as they might move to go about, but might not approach nearer: so as the boats stood all as in a theatre, beholding this light as an heavenly sign. It so fell out, that there was in one of the boats one of the wise men, of the society of Salomon's House; which house, or college (my good brethren) is the very eye of this kingdom; who having awhile attentively and devoutly viewed and contemplated this pillar and cross, fell down upon his face; and then raised himself upon his knees, and lifting up his hands to heaven, made his prayers in this manner.

"'LORD God of heaven and earth, thou hast vouchsafed of thy grace to those of our order, to know thy works of Creation, and the secrets of them: and to discern (as far as appertaineth to the generations of men) between divine miracles, works of nature, works of art, and impostures and illusions of all sorts. I do here acknowledge and testify before this people, that the thing which we now see before our eyes is thy Finger and a true Miracle. And forasmuch as we learn in our books that thou never workest miracles, but to divine and excellent end, (for the laws of nature are thine own laws, and thou exceedest them not but upon great cause,) we most humbly beseech thee to prosper this great sign, and to give us the interpretation and use of it in mercy; which thou dost in some part secretly promise by sending it unto us.'

"When he had made his prayer, he presently found the boat he was in, moveable and unbound; whereas all the rest remained still fast; and taking that for an assurance of leave to approach, he caused the boat to be softly and with silence rowed towards the pillar. But ere he came near it, the pillar and cross of light brake up, and cast itself abroad, as it were, into a firmament of many stars; which also vanished soon after, and there was nothing left to be seen, but a small ark, or chest of cedar, dry, and not wet at all with water, though it swam. And in the fore-end of it, which was towards him, grew a small green branch of palm; and when the wise man had taken it, with all reverence, into his boat, it opened of itself, and there were found in it a Book and a Letter; both written in fine parchment, and wrapped in sindons of linen. The Book contained all the canonical books of the Old and New Testament, according as you have them; (for we know well what the churches with you receive); and the Apocalypse itself, and some other books of the New Testament, which were not at that time written, were nevertheless in the Book. And for the Letter, it was in these words:

"'I, Bartholomew, a servant of the Highest, and Apostle of Jesus Christ, was warned by an angel that appeareth to me, in a vision of glory, that I should commit this ark to the floods of the sea. Therefore I do testify and declare unto that people where God shall ordain this ark to come to land, that in the same day is come unto them salvation and peace and good-will, from the Father, and from the Lord Jesus.'

"There was also in both these writings, as well the Book, as the Letter, wrought a great miracle, conform to that of the Apostles, in the original Gift of Tongues. For there being at that time in this land Hebrews, Persians, and Indians, besides the natives, every one read upon the Book, and Letter, as if they had been written in his own language. And thus was this land saved from infidelity (as the remainder of the old world was from water) by an ark, through the apostolical and miraculous evangelism of Saint Bartholomew." And here he paused, and a messenger came, and called him from us. So this was all that passed in that conference.

The next day, the same governor came again to us, immediately after dinner, and excused himself, saying; "That the day before he was called from us, somewhat abruptly, but now he would make us amends, and spend time with us if we held his company and conference agreeable." We answered, "That we held it so agreeable and pleasing to us, as we forgot both dangers past and fears to come, for the time we hear him speak; and that we thought an hour spent with him, was worth years of our former life." He bowed himself a little to us, and after we were set again, he said; "Well, the questions are on your part."

One of our number said, after a little pause; that there was a matter, we were no less desirous to know, than fearful to ask, lest we might presume too far. But encouraged by his rare humanity towards us, (that could scarce think ourselves strangers, being his vowed and professed servants,) we would take the hardiness to propound it: humbly beseeching him, if he thought it not fit to be answered, that he would pardon it, though he rejected it. We said; "We well observed those his words, which he formerly spake, that this happy island, where we now stood, was known to few, and yet knew most of the nations of the world; which we found to be true, considering they had the languages of Europe, and knew much of our state and business; and yet we in Europe, (notwithstanding all the remote discoveries and navigations of this last age), never heard of the least inkling or glimpse of this island. This we found wonderful strange; for that all nations have inter-knowledge one of another, either by voyage into foreign parts, or by strangers that come to them: and though the traveller into a foreign country, doth commonly know more by the eye, than he that stayeth at home can by relation of the traveller; yet both ways suffice to make a mutual knowledge, in some degree, on both parts. But for this island, we never heard tell of any ship of theirs that had been seen to arrive upon any shore of Europe; nor of either the East or West Indies; nor yet of any ship of any other part of the world, that had made return from them. And yet the marvel rested not in this. For the situation of it (as his lordship said) in the secret conclave of such a vast sea might cause it. But then, that they should have knowledge of the languages, books, affairs, of those that lie such a distance from them, it was a thing we could not tell what to make of; for that it seemed to us a conditioner and propriety of divine powers and beings, to be hidden and unseen to others, and yet to have others open and as in a light to them."

At this speech the Governor gave a gracious smile, and said; "That we did well to ask pardon for this question we now asked: for that it imported, as if we thought this land, a land of magicians, that sent forth spirits of the air into all parts, to bring them news and intelligence of other countries." It was answered by us all, in all possible humbleness, but yet with a countenance taking knowledge, that we knew that he spake it but merrily, "That we were apt enough to think there was somewhat supernatural in this island; but yet rather as angelical than magical. But to let his lordship know truly what it was that made us tender and doubtful to ask this question, it was not any such conceit," but because we remembered, he had given a touch in his former speech, that this land had laws of secrecy touching strangers." To this he said; "You remember it aright and therefore in that I shall say to you, I must reserve some particulars, which it is not lawful for me to reveal; but there will be enough left, to give you satisfaction.

"You shall understand (that which perhaps you will scarce think credible) that about three thousand years ago, or somewhat more, the navigation of the world, (especially for remote voyages,) was greater than at this day. Do not think with yourselves, that I know not how much it is increased with you, within these six-score years: I know it well: and yet I say greater then than now; whether it was, that the example of the ark, that saved the remnant of men from the universal deluge, gave men confidence to adventure upon the waters; or what it was; but such is the truth. The Phoenicians, and especially the Tyrians, had great fleets. So had the Carthaginians their colony, which is yet further west. Toward the east the shipping of Egypt and of Palestine was likewise great. China also, and the great Atlantis, (that you call America,) which have now but junks and canoes, abounded then in tall ships. This island, (as appeareth by faithful registers of those times,) had then fifteen hundred strong ships, of great content. Of all this, there is with you sparing memory, or none; but we have large knowledge thereof.

"At that time, this land was known and frequented by the ships and vessels of all the nations before named. And (as it cometh to pass) they had many times men of other countries, that were no sailors, that came with them; as Persians, Chaldeans, Arabians; so as almost all nations of might and fame resorted hither; of whom we have some stirps, and little tribes with us at this day. And for our own ships, they went sundry voyages, as well to your straits, which you call the Pillars of Hercules, as to other parts in the Atlantic and

Mediterrane Seas; as to Paguin, (which is the same with Cambaline,) and Quinzy, upon the Oriental Seas, as far as to the borders of the East Tartary.

"At the same time, and an age after, or more, the inhabitants of the great Atlantis did flourish. For though the narration and description, which is made by a great man with you; that the descendants of Neptune planted there; and of the magnificent temple, palace, city, and hill; and the manifold streams of goodly navigable rivers, (which as so many chains environed the same site and temple); and the several degrees of ascent, whereby men did climb up to the same, as if it had been a *scala coeli*, be all poetical and fabulous: yet so much is true, that the said country of Atlantis, as well that of Peru, then called Coya, as that of Mexico, then named Tyrambel, were mighty and proud kingdoms in arms, shipping and riches: so mighty, as at one time (or at least within the space of ten years) they both made two great expeditions; they of Tyrambel through the Atlantic to the Mediterrane Sea; and they of Coya through the South Sea upon this our island: and for the former of these, which was into Europe, the same author amongst you (as it seemeth) had some relation from the Egyptian priest whom he cited. For assuredly such a thing there was. But whether it were the ancient Athenians that had the glory of the repulse and resistance of those forces, I can say nothing: but certain it is, there never came back either ship or man from that voyage. Neither had the other voyage of those of Coya upon us had better fortune, if they had not met with enemies of greater clemency. For the king of this island, (by name Altabin,) a wise man and a great warrior, knowing well both his own strength and that of his enemies, handled the matter so, as he cut off their land-forces from their ships; and entoiled both their navy and their tamp with a greater power than theirs, both by sea and land: arid compelled them to render themselves without striking stroke and after they were at his mercy, contenting himself only with their oath that they should no more bear arms against him, dismissed them all in safety.

"But the divine revenge overtook not long after those proud enterprises. For within less than the space of one hundred years, the great Atlantis was utterly lost and destroyed: not by a great earthquake, as your man saith; (for that whole tract is little subject to earthquakes;) but by a particular' deluge or inundation; those countries having, at this day, far greater rivers and far higher mountains to pour down waters, than any part of the old world. But it is true that the same inundation was not deep; not past forty foot, in most places, from the ground; so that although it destroyed man and beast generally, yet some few wild inhabitants of the wood escaped. Birds also were saved by flying to the high trees and woods. For as for men, although they had buildings in many places, higher than the depth of the water, yet that inundation, though it were shallow, had a long continuance; whereby they of the vale that were not drowned, perished for want of food and other things necessary.

"So as marvel you not at the thin population of America, nor at the rudeness and ignorance of the people; for you must account your inhabitants of America as a young people; younger a thousand years, at the least, than the rest of the world: for that there was so much time between the universal flood and their particular inundation. For the poor remnant of human seed, which remained in their mountains, peopled the country again slowly, by little and little; and being simple and savage people, (not like Noah and his sons, which was the chief family of the earth;) they were not able to leave letters, arts, and civility to their posterity; and having likewise in their mountainous habitations been used (in respect of the extreme cold of those regions) to clothe themselves with the skins of tigers, bears, and great hairy goats, that they have in those parts; when after they came down into the valley, and found the intolerable heats which are there, and knew no means of lighter apparel, they were forced to begin the custom of going naked, which continueth at this day. Only they take great pride and delight in the feathers of birds; and this also they took from those their ancestors of the mountains, who were invited unto it by the infinite flights of birds that came up to the high grounds, while the waters stood below. So you see, by this main accident of time, we lost our traffic with the Americans, with whom of, all others, in regard they lay nearest to us, we had most commerce.

"As for the other parts of the world, it is most manifest that in the ages following (whether it were in respect of wars, or by a natural revolution of time,) navigation did every where greatly decay; and specially far voyages (the rather by the use of galleys, and such vessels as could hardly brook the ocean,) were altogether left and omitted. So then, that part of intercourse which could be from other nations to sail to us, you see how it hath long since ceased; except it were by some rare accident, as this of yours. But now of the cessation of that other part of intercourse, which might be by our sailing to other nations, I must yield you some other cause. For I cannot say (if

I shall say truly,) but our shipping, for number, strength, mariners, pilots, and all things that appertain to navigation, is as great as ever; and therefore why we should sit at home, I shall now give you an account by itself: and it will draw nearer to give you satisfaction to your principal question.

"There reigned in this land, about nineteen hundred years ago, a king, whose memory of all others we most adore; not superstitiously, but as a divine instrument, though a mortal man; his name was Solamona: and we esteem him as the lawgiver of our nation. This king had a large heart, inscrutable for good; and was wholly bent to make his kingdom and people happy. He therefore, taking into consideration how sufficient and substantive this land was to maintain itself without any aid (at all) of the foreigner; being five thousand six hundred miles in circuit, and of rare fertility of soil in the greatest part thereof; and finding also the shipping of this country might be plentifully set on work, both by fishing and by transportations from port to port, and likewise by sailing unto some small islands that are not far from us, and are under the crown and laws of this state; and, recalling into his memory the happy and flourishing estate wherein this land then was; so as it might be a thousand ways altered to the worse, but scarce any one way to the better; thought nothing wanted to his noble and heroical intentions, but only (as far as human foresight might reach) to give perpetuity to that which was in his time so happily established. Therefore amongst his other fundamental laws of this kingdom, he did ordain the interdicts and prohibitions which we have touching entrance of strangers; which at that time (though it was after the calamity of America) was frequent; doubting novelties, and commixture of manners. It is true, the like law against the admission of strangers without licence is an ancient law in the kingdom of China, and yet continued in use. But there it is a poor thing; and hath made them a curious, ignorant, fearful, foolish nation. But our lawgiver made his law of another temper. For first, he hath preserved all points of humanity, in taking order and making provision for the relief of strangers distressed; whereof you have tasted."

At which speech (as reason was) we all rose up and bowed ourselves. He went on.

"That king also, still desiring to join humanity and policy together; and thinking it against humanity, to detain strangers here against their wills, and against policy that they should return and discover their knowledge of this estate, he took this course: he did ordain that of the strangers that should be permitted to land, as many (at all times) might depart as would; but as many as would stay should have very good conditions and means to live from the state. Wherein he saw so far, that now in so many ages since the prohibition, we have memory not of one ship that ever returned, and but of thirteen persons only, at several times, that chose to return in our bottoms. What those few that returned may have reported abroad I know not. But you must think, whatsoever they have said could be taken where they came but for a dream. Now for our travelling from henna into parts abroad, our Lawgiver thought fit altogether to restrain it. So is it not in China. For the Chinese sail where they will or can; which sheweth that their law of keeping out strangers is a law of pusillanimity and fear. But this restraint of ours hath one only exception, which is admirable; preserving the good which cometh by communicating with strangers, and avoiding the hurt; and I will now open it to you. And here I shall seem a little to digress, but you will by and by find it pertinent.

"Ye shall understand (my dear friends) that amongst the excellent acts of that king, one above all hath the pre-eminence. It was the erection and institution of an Order or Society, which we call Salomon's House; the noblest foundation (as we think) that ever was upon the earth; and the lanthorn of this kingdom. It is dedicated to the study of the works and creatures of God. Some think it beareth the founder's name a little corrupted, as if it should be Solamona's House. But the records write it as it is spoken. So as I take it to be denominate of the king of the Hebrews, which is famous with you, and no stranger to us. For we have some parts of his works, which with you are lost; namely, that natural history, which he wrote, of all plants, from the cedar of Libanus to the moss that groweth out of the wall, and of all things that have life and motion. This maketh me think that our king, finding himself to symbolize in many things with that king of the Hebrews (which lived many years before him), honoured him with the title of this foundation. And I am rather induced to be of this opinion, for that I find in ancient records this Order or Society is sometimes called Salomon's House, and sometimes the College of the Six Days Works; whereby I am satisfied that our excellent king had learned from the Hebrews that God had created the world and all that therein is within six days: and therefore he instituting that House for the finding out of the true nature of all things, (whereby God might have the more glory in the workmanship of them, and insert the more fruit in the use of them), did give it also that second name.

"But now to come to our present purpose. When the king had forbidden to all his people navigation into any part that was not under his crown, he made nevertheless this ordinance; that every twelve years there should be set forth, out of this kingdom two ships, appointed to several voyages; That in either of these ships there should be a mission of three of the Fellows or Brethren of Salomon's House; whose errand was only to give us knowledge of the affairs and state of those countries to which they were designed, and especially of the sciences, arts, manufactures, and inventions of all the world; and withal to bring unto us books, instruments, and patterns in every kind: That the ships, after they had landed the brethren, should return; and that the brethren should stay abroad till the new mission. These ships are not otherwise fraught, than with store of victuals, and good quantity of treasure to remain with the brethren, for the buying of such things and rewarding of such persons as they should think fit. Now for me to tell you how the vulgar sort of mariners are contained from being discovered at land; and how they that must be put on shore for any time, colour themselves under the names of other nations; and to what places these voyages have been designed; and what places of rendezvous are appointed for the new missions; and the like circumstances of the practique; I may not do it: neither is it much to your desire. But thus you see we maintain a trade not for gold, silver, or jewels; nor for silks; nor for spices; nor any other commodity of matter; but only for God's first creature, which was Light: to have light (I say) of the growth of all parts of the world."

And when he had said this, he was silent; and so were we all. For indeed we were all astonished to hear so strange things so probably told. And he, perceiving that we were willing to say somewhat but had it not ready in great courtesy took us off, and descended to ask us questions of our voyage and fortunes and in the end concluded, that we might do well to think with ourselves what time of stay we would demand of the state; and bade us not to scant ourselves; for he would procure such time as we desired: Whereupon we all rose up, and presented ourselves to kiss the skirt of his tippet; but he would not suffer us; and so took his leave. But when it came once amongst our people that the state used to offer conditions to strangers that would stay, we had work enough to get any of our men to look to our ship; and to keep them from going presently to the governor to crave conditions. But with much ado we refrained them, till we might agree what course to take.

We took ourselves now for free men, seeing there was no danger of our utter perdition; and lived most joyfully, going abroad and seeing what was to be seen in the city and places adjacent within our tedder; and obtaining acquaintance with many of the city, not of the meanest quality; at whose hands we found such humanity, and such a freedom and desire to take strangers as it were into their bosom, as was enough to make us forget all that was dear to us in our own countries: and continually we met with many things right worthy of observation and relation: as indeed, if there be a mirror in the world worthy to hold men's eyes, it is that country.

One day there were two of our company bidden to a Feast of the Family, as they call it. A most natural, pious, and reverend custom it is, shewing that nation to be compounded of all goodness. This is the manner of it. It is granted to any man that shall live to see thirty persons descended of his body alive together, and all above three years old, to make this feast which is done at the cost of the state. The Father of the Family, whom they call the Tirsan, two days before the feast, taketh to him three of such friends as he liketh to choose; and is assisted also by the governor of the city or place where the feast is celebrated; and all the persons of the family, of both sexes, are summoned to attend him. These two days the Tirsan sitteth in consultation concerning the good estate of the family. There, if there be any discord or suits between any of the family, they are compounded and appeased. There, if any of the family be distressed or decayed, order is taken for their relief and competent means to live. There, if any be subject to vice, or take ill courses, they are reproved and censured. So likewise direction is given touching marriages, and the courses of life, which any of them should take, with divers other the like orders and advices. The governor assisteth, to the end to put in execution by his public authority the decrees and orders of the Tirsan, if they should be disobeyed; though that seldom needeth; such reverence and obedience they give to the order of nature. The Tirsan doth also then ever choose one man from among his sons, to live in house with him; who is called ever after the Son of the Vine. The reason will hereafter appear.

On the feast day, the father or Tirsan cometh forth after divine service into a large room where the feast is celebrated; which room hath an half-pace at the upper end. Against the wall, in the middle of the half-pace, is a chair placed for him, with a table and carpet before it. Over the chair is a state, made round or oval, and it is of ivy; an ivy somewhat whiter than ours, like the leaf of a silver asp; but more shining; for it is green all winter. And the state is curiously wrought with silver and silk of divers colours, broiding or binding in the ivy; and is ever of the work of some of the daughters of the family; and veiled over at the top with a fine net of silk and silver. But the substance of it is true ivy; whereof, after it is taken down, the friends of the family are desirous to have some leaf or sprig to keep.

The Tirsan cometh forth with all his generation or linage, the males before him, and the females following him; and if there be a mother from whose body the whole linage is descended, there is a traverse placed in a loft above on the right hand of the chair, with a privy door, and a carved window of glass, leaded with gold and blue; where she sitteth, but is not seen. When the Tirsan is come forth, he sitteth down in the chair; and all the linage place themselves against the wall, both at his back and upon the return of the half-pace, in order of their years without difference of sex; and stand upon their feet. When he is set; the room being always full of company, but well kept and without disorder; after some pause, there cometh in from the lower end of the room, a taratan (which is as much as an herald) and on either side of him two young lads; whereof one carrieth a scroll of their shining yellow parchment; and the other a cluster of grapes of gold, with a long foot or stalk. The herald and children are clothed with mantles of sea-water green satin; but the herald's mantle is streamed with gold, and hath a train.

Then the herald with three curtesies, or rather inclinations, cometh up as far as the half-pace; and there first taketh into his hand the scroll. This scroll is the king's charter, containing gifts of revenew, and many privileges, exemptions, and points of honour, granted to the Father of the Family; and is ever styled and directed, To such do one our well beloved friend and creditor: which is a title proper only to this case. For they say the king is debtor to no man, but for propagation of his subjects. The seal set to the king's charter is the king's image, imbossed or moulded in gold; and though such charters be expedited of course, and as of right, yet they are varied by discretion, according to the number and dignity of the family. This charter the herald readeth aloud; and while it is read, the father or Tirsan standeth up supported by two of his sons, such as he chooseth. Then the herald mounteth the half-pace and delivereth the charter into his hand: and with that there is an acclamation by all that are present in their language, which is thus much: Happy are the people of Bensalem.

Then the herald taketh into his hand from the other child the cluster of grapes, which is of gold, both the stalk and the grapes. But the grapes are daintily enamelled; and if the males of the family be the greater number, the grapes are enamelled purple, with a little sun set on the top; if the females, then they are enamelled into a greenish yellow, with a crescent on the top. The grapes are in number as many as there are descendants of the family. This golden cluster the herald delivereth also to the Tirsan; who presently delivereth it over to that son that he had formerly chosen to be in house with him: who beareth it before his father as an ensign of honour when he goeth in public, ever after; and is thereupon called the Son of the Vine.

After the ceremony endeth the father or Tirsan retireth; and after some time cometh forth again to dinner, where he sitteth alone under the state, as before; and none of his descendants sit with him, of what degree or dignity soever, except he hap to be of Salomon's House. He is served only by his own children, such as are male; who perform unto him all service of the table upon the knee; and the women only stand about him, leaning against the wall. The room below the half-pace hath tables on the sides for the guests that are bidden; who are served with great and comely order; and towards the end of dinner (which in the greatest feasts with them lasteth never above an hour and an half) there is an hymn sung, varied according to the invention of him that composeth it (for they have excellent posy) but the subject of it is (always) the praises of Adam and Noah and Abraham; whereof the former two peopled the world, and the last was the Father of the Faithful: concluding ever with a thanksgiving for the nativity of our Saviour, in whose birth the births of all are only blessed.

Dinner being done, the Tirsan retireth again; and having withdrawn himself alone into a place, where he makes some private prayers, he cometh forth the third time, to give the blessing with all his descendants, who stand about him as at the first. Then he calleth them forth by one and by one, by name, as he pleaseth, though seldom the order of age be inverted. The person that is called (the table being before removed) kneeleth down before the chair, and the father layeth his hand upon his head, or her head, and giveth the blessing in these words:

Son of Bensalem, (or daughter of Bensalem,) thy father with it: the man by whom thou hast breath and life speaketh the word: the blessing of the everlasting Father, the Prince of Peace, and the Holy Dove, be upon thee, and make the days of thy pilgrimage good and many.

This he saith to every of them; and that done, if there be any of his sons of eminent merit and virtue, (so they be not above two,) he calleth for them again; and saith, laying his arm over their shoulders, they standing:

Sons, it is well ye are born, give God the praise, and persevere to the end.

And withall delivereth to either of them a jewel, made in the figure of an ear of wheat, which they ever after wear in the front of their turban or hat. This done, they fall to music and dances, and other recreations, after their manner, for the rest of the day. This is the full order of that feast.

By that time six or seven days were spent, I was fallen into straight acquaintance with a merchant of that city, whose name was Joabin. He was a Jew and circumcised: for they have some few stirps of Jews yet remaining among them, whom they leave to their own religion. Which they may the better do, because they are of a far differing disposition from the Jews in other parts. For whereas they hate the name of Christ; and have a secret inbred rancour against the people among whom they live: these (contrariwise) give unto our Saviour many high attributes, and love the nation of Bensalem extremely. Surely this man of whom I speak would ever acknowledge that Christ was born of a virgin and that he was more than a man; and he would tell how God made him ruler of the seraphims which guard his throne; and they call him also the Milken Way, and the Eliah of the Messiah; and many other high names; which though they be inferior to his divine majesty, yet they are far from the language of other Jews.

And for the country of Bensalem, this man would make no end of commending it; being desirous, by tradition among the Jews there, to have it believed that the people thereof were of the generations of Abraham, by another son, whom they call Nachoran; and that Moses by a secret Cabala ordained the Laws of Bensalem which they now use; and that when the Messiah should come, and sit in his throne at Hierusalem, the king of Bensalem should sit at his feet, whereas other kings should keep a great distance. But yet setting aside these Jewish dreams, the man was a wise man, and learned, and of great policy, and excellently seen in the laws and customs of that nation.

Amongst other discourses, one day I told him I was much affected with the relation I had, from some of the company, of their custom, in holding the Feast of the Family; for that (methought) I had never heard of a solemnity wherein nature did so much preside. And because propagation of families proceedeth from the nuptial copulation, I desired to know of him what laws and customs they had concerning marriage; and whether they kept marriage well and whether they were tied to one wife; for that where population is so much affected,' and such as with them it seemed to be, there is commonly permission of plurality of wives.

To this he said, "You have reason for to commend that excellent institution of the Feast of the Family. And indeed we have experience that those families that are partakers of the blessing of that feast do flourish and prosper ever after in an extraordinary manner. But hear me now, and I will tell you what I know. You shall understand that there is not under the heavens so chaste a nation as this of Bensalem; nor so free from all pollution or foulness. It is the virgin of the world. I remember I have read in one of your European books, of an holy hermit amongst you that desired to see the Spirit of Fornication; and there appeared to him a little foul ugly Æthiop. But if he had desired to see the Spirit of Chastity of Bensalem, it would have appeared to him in the likeness of a fair beautiful Cherubim. For there is nothing amongst mortal men more fair and admirable, than the chaste minds of this people. Know therefore, that with them there are no stews, no dissolute houses, no courtesans, nor anything of that kind. Nay they wonder (with detestation) at you in Europe, which permit such things. They say ye have put marriage out of office: for marriage is ordained a remedy for unlawful concupiscence; and natural concupiscence seemeth as a spar to marriage. But when men have at hand a remedy more agreeable to their corrupt will, marriage is almost expulsed. And therefore there are with you seen infinite men that marry not, but chose rather a libertine and impure single life, than to be yoked in marriage; and many that do marry, marry late, when the prime and strength of their years is past. And when they do marry, what is marriage to them but a very bargain; wherein is sought alliance, or portion, or reputation, with some desire (almost indifferent) of issue; and not the faithful nuptial union of man and wife, that was first instituted. Neither is it possible that those that have cast away so basely so much of their strength, should greatly esteem children, (being of the same matter,) as chaste men do. So likewise during marriage, is the case much amended, as it ought to be if those things were tolerated only for necessity? No, but they remain still as a very affront to marriage. The haunting of those dissolute places, or resort to courtesans, are no more punished in married men than in bachelors. And the depraved custom of change, and the delight in meretricious embracements, (where sin is turned into art,) maketh marriage a dull thing, and a kind of imposition or tax. They hear you defend these things, as done to avoid greater evils; as advoutries, deflowering of virgins, unnatural lust, and the like. But they say this is a preposterous wisdom; and they call it Lot's offer, who to save his guests from abusing, offered his daughters: nay they say farther that there is little gained in this; for that the same vices and appetites do still remain and abound; unlawful lust being like a furnace, that if you stop the flames altogether, it will quench; but if you give it any vent, it will rage. As for masculine love, they have no touch of it; and yet there are not so faithful and inviolate friendships in the world again as are there; and to speak generally, (as I said before,) I have not read of any such chastity, in any people as theirs. And their usual saying is, That whosoever is unchaste cannot reverence himself; and they say, That the reverence of a man's self, is, next to religion, the chiefest bridle of all vices."

And when he had said this, the good Jew paused a little; whereupon I, far more willing to hear him speak on than to speak myself, yet thinking it decent that upon his pause of speech I should not be altogether silent, said only this; "That I would say to him, as the widow of Sarepta said to Elias; that he was come to bring to memory our sins; and that I confess the righteousness of Bensalem was greater than the righteousness of Europe." At which speech he bowed his head, and went on in this manner:

"They have also many wise and excellent laws touching marriage. They allow no polygamy. They have ordained that none do intermarry or contract, until a month be past from their first interview. Marriage without consent of parents they do not make void, but they mulct it in the inheritors: for the children of such marriages are not admitted to inherit above a third part of their parents' inheritance. I have read in a book of one of your men, of a

Feigned Commonwealth, where the married couple are permitted, before they contract, to see one another naked. This they dislike; for they think it a scorn to give a refusal after so familiar knowledge: but because of many hidden defects in men and women's bodies, they have a more civil way; for they have near every town a couple of pools, (which they call Adam and Eve's pools,) where it is permitted to one of the friends of the men, and another of the friends of the woman, to see them severally bathe naked."

And as we were thus in conference, there came one that seemed to be a messenger, in a rich huke, that spake with the Jew: whereupon he turned to me and said; "You will pardon me, for I am commanded away in haste." The next morning he came to me again, joyful as it seemed, and said; "There is word come to the Governor of the city, that one of the Fathers of Salomon's House will be here this day seven-night: we have seen none of them this dozen years. His coming is in state; but the cause of his coming is secret. I will provide you and your fellows of a good standing to see his entry." I thanked him, and told him, I was most glad of the news.

The day being come, he made his entry. He was a man of middle stature and age, comely of person, and had an aspect as if he pitied men. He was clothed in a robe of fine black cloth, with wide sleeves and a cape. His under garment was of excellent white linen down to the foot, girt with a girdle of the same; and a sindon or tippet of the same about his neck. He had gloves, that were curious, and set with stone; and shoes of peach-coloured velvet. His neck was bare to the shoulders. His hat was like a helmet, or Spanish montera; and his locks curled below it decently: they were of colour brown. His beard was cut round, and of the same colour with his hair, somewhat lighter. He was carried in a rich chariot without wheels, litter-wise; with two horses at either end, richly trapped in blue velvet embroidered; and two footmen on each side in the like attire. The chariot was all of cedar, gilt, and adorned with crystal; save that the fore-end had panels of sapphires, set in borders of gold; and the hinder-end the like of emeralds of the Peru colour. There was also a sun of gold, radiant, upon the top, in the midst; and on the top before, a small cherub of gold, with wings displayed. The chariot was covered with cloth of gold tissued upon blue. He had before him fifty attendants, young men all, in white satin loose coats to the mid leg; and stockings of white silk; and shoes of blue velvet; and hats of blue velvet; with fine plumes of diverse colours, set round like hat-bands. Next before the chariot, went two men, bare-headed, in linen garments down the foot, girt, and shoes of blue velvet; who carried, the one a crosier, the other a pastoral staff like a sheep-hook; neither of them of metal, but the crosier of balm-wood, the pastoral staff of cedar. Horsemen he had none, neither before nor behind his chariot: as it seemeth, to avoid all tumult and trouble. Behind his chariot went all the officers and principals of the companies of the city. He sat alone, upon cushions of a kind of excellent plush, blue; and under his foot curious carpets of silk of diverse colours, like the Persian, but far finer. He held up his bare hand as he went, as blessing the people, but in silence. The street was wonderfully well kept: so that there was never any army had their men stand in better battle-array than the people stood. The windows likewise were not crowded, but every one stood in them as if they had been placed.

When the shew was past, the Jew said to me; "I shall not be able to attend you as I would, in regard of some charge the city hath laid upon me, for the entertaining of this great person." Three days after the Jew came to me again, and said; "Ye are happy men; for the Father of Salomon's House taketh knowledge of your being here, and commanded me to tell you that he will admit all your company to his presence, and have private conference with one of you, that ye shall choose: and for this hath appointed the next day after to-morrow. And because he meaneth to give you his blessing, he hath appointed it in the forenoon."

We came at our day and hour, and I was chosen by my fellows for the private access. We found him in a fair chamber, richly hanged, and carpeted under foot without any degrees to the state. He was set upon a low Throne richly adorned, and a rich cloth of state over his head, of blue satin embroidered. He was alone, save that he had two pages of honour, on either hand one, finely attired in white. His under garments were the like that we saw him wear in the chariot; but instead of his gown, he had on him a mantle with a cape, of the same fine black, fastened about him. When we came in, as we were taught, we bowed low at our first entrance; and when we were come near his chair, he stood up, holding forth his hand ungloved, and in posture of blessing; and we every one of us stooped down, and kissed the hem of his tippet. That done, the rest departed, and I remained. Then he warned the pages forth of the room, and caused me to sit down beside him, and spake to me thus in the Spanish tongue.

"God bless thee, my son; I will give thee the greatest jewel I have. For I will impart unto thee, for the love of God and men, a relation of the true state of Salomon's House. Son, to make you know the true state of Salomon's House, I will keep this order. First, I will set forth unto you the end of our foundation. Secondly, the preparations and instruments we have for our works. Thirdly, the several employments and functions whereto our fellows are assigned. And fourthly, the ordinances and rites which we observe.

"The end of our foundation is the knowledge of causes, and secret motions of things; and the enlarging of the bounds of human empire, to the effecting of all things possible.

"The Preparations and Instruments are these. We have large and deep caves of several depths: the deepest are sunk six hundred fathom: and some of them are digged and made under great hills and mountains: so that if you reckon together the depth of the hill and the depth of the cave, they are (some of them) above three miles deep. For we find, that the depth of a hill, and the depth of a cave from the flat, is the same thing; both remote alike, from the sun and heaven's beams, and from the open air. These caves we call the Lower Region; and we use them for all coagulations, indurations, refrigerations, and conservations of bodies. We use them likewise for the imitation of natural mines; and the producing also of new artificial metals, by compositions and materials which we use, and lay there for many years. We use them also sometimes, (which may seem strange,) for curing of some diseases, and for prolongation of life in some hermits that choose to live there, well accommodated of all things necessary, and indeed live very long; by whom also we learn many things.

"We have burials in several earths, where we put diverse cements, as the Chineses do their porcellain. But we have them in greater variety, and some of them more fine. We have also great variety of composts and soils, for the making of the earth fruitful.

"We have high towers; the highest about half a mile in height; and some of them likewise set upon high mountains; so that the vantage of the hill with the tower is in the highest of them three miles at least. And these places we call the Upper Region; accounting the air between the high places and the low, as a Middle Region. We use these towers, according to their several heights, and situations, for insolation, refrigeration, conservation; and for the view of divers meteors; as winds, rain, snow, hail; and some of the fiery meteors also. And upon them, in some places, are dwellings of hermits, whom we visit sometimes, and instruct what to observe.

"We have great lakes, both salt, and fresh; whereof we have use for the fish and fowl. We use them also for burials of some natural bodies: for we find a difference in things buried in earth or in air below the earth, and things buried in water. We have also pools, of which some do strain fresh water out of salt; and others by art do turn fresh water into salt. We have also some rocks in the midst of the sea, and some bays upon the shore for some works, wherein is required the air and vapor of the sea. We have likewise violent streams and cataracts, which serve us for many motions: and likewise engines for multiplying and enforcing of winds, to set also on going diverse motions.

"We have also a number of artificial wells and fountains, made in imitation of the natural sources and baths; as tincted upon vitriol, sulphur, steel, brass, lead, nitre, and other minerals. And again we have little wells for infusions of many things, where the waters take the virtue quicker and better, than in vessels or basins. And amongst them we have a water which we call Water of Paradise, being, by that we do to it made very sovereign for health, and prolongation of life.

"We have also great and spacious houses where we imitate and demonstrate meteors; as snow, hail, rain, some artificial rains of bodies and not of water, thunders, lightnings; also generations of bodies in air; as frogs, flies, and divers others.

"We have also certain chambers, which we call Chambers of Health, where we qualify the air as we think good and proper for the cure of divers diseases, and preservation of health.

"We have also fair and large baths, of several mixtures, for the cure of diseases, and the restoring of man's body from arefaction: and others for the confirming of it in strength of sinewes, vital parts, and the very juice and substance of the body.

"We have also large and various orchards and gardens; wherein we do not so much respect beauty, as variety of ground and soil, proper for divers trees and herbs: and some very spacious, where trees and berries are set whereof we make divers kinds of drinks, besides the vineyards. In these we practise likewise all conclusions of grafting, and inoculating as well of wild-trees as fruit-trees, which produceth many effects. And we make (by art) in the same orchards and gardens, trees and flowers to come earlier or later than their seasons; and to come up and bear more speedily than by their natural course they do. We make them also by art greater much than their nature; and their fruit greater and sweeter and of differing taste, smell, colour, and figure, from their nature. And many of them we so order, as they become of medicinal use.

"We have also means to make divers plants rise by mixtures of earths without seeds; and likewise to make divers new plants, differing from the vulgar; and to make one tree or plant turn into another.

"We have also parks and enclosures of all sorts of beasts and birds which we use not only for view or rareness, but likewise for dissections and trials; that thereby we may take light what may be wrought upon the body of man. Wherein we find many strange effects; as continuing life in them, though divers parts, which you account vital, be perished and taken forth; resuscitating of some that seem dead in appearance; and the like. We try also all poisons and other medicines upon them, as well of chirurgery, as physic. By art likewise, we make them greater or taller than their kind is; and contrariwise dwarf them, and stay their growth: we make them more fruitful and bearing than their kind is; and contrariwise barren and not generative. Also we make them differ in colour, shape, activity, many ways. We find means to make commixtures and copulations of different kinds; which have produced many new kinds, and them not barren, as the general opinion is. We make a number of kinds of serpents, worms, flies, fishes, of putrefaction; whereof some are advanced (in effect) to be perfect creatures, like bests or birds; and have sexes, and do propagate. Neither do we this by chance, but we know beforehand, of what matter and commixture what kind of those creatures will arise.

"We have also particular pools, where we make trials upon fishes, as we have said before of beasts and birds.

"We have also places for breed and generation of those kinds of worms and flies which are of special use; such as are with you your silk-worms and bees.

"I will not hold you long with recounting of our brewhouses, bake-houses, and kitchens, where are made divers drinks, breads, and meats, rare and of special effects. Wines we have of grapes; and drinks of other juice of fruits, of grains, and of roots; and of mixtures with honey, sugar, manna, and fruits dried, and decocted; Also of the tears or woundings of trees; and of the pulp of canes. And these drinks are of several ages, some to the age or last of forty years. We have drinks also brewed with several herbs, and roots, and spices; yea with several fleshes, and white-meats; whereof some of the drinks are such, as they are in effect meat and drink both: so that divers, especially in age, do desire to live with them, with little or no meat or bread. And above all, we strive to have drink of extreme thin parts, to insinuate into the body, and yet without all biting, sharpness, or fretting; insomuch as some of them put upon the back of your hand will, with a little stay, pass through to the palm, and yet taste mild to the mouth. We have also waters which we ripen in that fashion, as they become nourishing; so that they are indeed excellent drink; and.many will use no other. Breads we have of several grains, roots, and kernels; yea and some of flesh and fish dried; with divers kinds of leavenings and seasonings: so that some do extremely move appetites; some do nourish so, as divers do live of them, without any other meat; who live very long. So for meats, we have some of them so beaten and made tender and mortified,' yet without all corrupting, as a weak heat of the stomach will turn them into good chylus; as well as a strong heat would meat otherwise prepared. We have some meats also and breads and drinks, which taken by men enable them to fast long after; and some other, that used make the very flesh of men's bodies sensibly' more hard and tough and their strength far greater than otherwise it would be.

"We have dispensatories, or shops of medicines. Wherein you may easily think, if we have such variety of plants and living creatures more than you have in Europe, (for we know what you have,) the simples, drugs, and ingredients of medicines, must likewise be in so much the greater variety. We have them likewise of divers ages, and long fermentations. And for their preparations, we have not only all manner of exquisite distillations and separations, and especially by gentle heats and percolations through divers strainers, yea and substances; but also exact forms of composition, whereby they incorporate almost, as they were natural simples.

"We have also divers mechanical arts, which you have not; and stuffs made by them; as papers, linen, silks, tissues; dainty works of feathers of wonderful lustre; excellent dies, and, many others; and shops likewise, as well for such as are not brought into vulgar use amongst us as for those that are. For you must know that of the things before recited, many of them are grown into use throughout the kingdom; but yet, if they did flow from our invention, we have of them also for patterns and principals.

"We have also furnaces of great diversities, and that keep great diversity of heats; fierce and quick; strong and constant; soft and mild; blown, quiet; dry, moist; and the like. But above all, we have heats, in imitation of the Sun's and heavenly bodies' heats, that pass divers inequalities, and (as it were) orbs, progresses, and returns, whereby we produce admirable effects. Besides, we have heats of dungs; and of bellies and maws of living creatures, and of their bloods and bodies; and of hays and herbs laid up moist; of lime unquenched; and such like. Instruments also which generate heat only by motion. And farther, places for strong insulations; and again, places under the earth, which by nature, or art, yield heat. These divers heats we use, as the nature of the operation, which we intend, requireth.

"We have also perspective-houses, where we make demonstrations of all lights and radiations; and of all colours: and out of things uncoloured and transparent, we can represent unto you all several colours; not in rain-bows, (as it is in gems, and prisms,) but of themselves single. We represent also all multiplications of light, which we carry to great distance, and make so sharp as to discern small points and lines. Also all colourations of light; all delusions and deceits of the sight, in figures, magnitudes, motions, colours all demonstrations of shadows. We find also divers means, yet unknown to you, of producing of light originally from divers bodies. We procure means of seeing objects afar off; as in the heaven and remote places; and represent things near as afar off; and things afar off as near; making feigned distances. We have also helps for the sight, far above spectacles and glasses in use. We have also glasses and means to see small and minute bodies perfectly and distinctly; as the shapes and colours of small flies and worms, grains and flaws in gems, which cannot otherwise be seen, observations in urine and blood not otherwise to be seen. We make artificial rain-bows, halo's, and circles about light. We represent also all manner of reflexions, refractions, and multiplications of visual beams of objects.

"We have also precious stones of all kinds, many of them of great beauty, and to you unknown; crystals likewise; and glasses of divers kinds; and amongst them some of metals vitrificated, and other materials besides those of which you make glass. Also a number of fossils, and imperfect minerals, which you have not. Likewise loadstones of prodigious virtue; and other rare stones, both natural and artificial.

"We have also sound-houses, where we practise and demonstrate all sounds, and their generation. We have harmonies which you have not, of quarter-sounds, and lesser slides of sounds. Divers instruments of music likewise to you unknown, some sweeter than any you have, together with bells and rings that are dainty and sweet. We represent small sounds as great and deep; likewise great sounds extenuate and sharp; we make divers tremblings and warblings of sounds, which in their original are entire. We represent and imitate all articulate sounds and letters, and the voices and notes of beasts and birds. We have certain helps which set to the ear do further the hearing greatly. We have also divers strange and artificial echoes, reflecting the voice many times, and as it were tossing it: and some that give back the voice louder than it came, some shriller, and some deeper; yea, some rendering the voice differing in the letters or articulate sound from that they receive. We have also means to convey sounds in trunks and pipes, in strange lines and distances.

"We have also perfume-houses; wherewith we join also practices of taste. We multiply smells, which may seem strange. We imitate smells, making all smells to breathe outs of other mixtures than those that give them. We make divers imitations of taste likewise, so that they will deceive any man's taste. And in this house we contain also a confiture-house; where we make all sweet-meats, dry and moist; and divers pleasant wines, milks, broths, and sallets; in far greater variety than you have.

"We have also engine-houses, where are prepared engines and instruments for all sorts of motions. There we imitate and practise to make swifter motions than any you have, either out of your muskets or any engine that you have: and to make them and multiply them more easily, and with small force, by wheels and other means: and to make them stronger and more violent than yours are; exceeding your greatest cannons and basilisks. We represent also ordnance and instruments of war, and engines of all kinds: and likewise new mixtures and compositions of gun-powder, wild-fires burning in water, and unquenchable. Also fireworks of all variety both for pleasure and use. We imitate also flights of birds; we have some degrees of flying in the air. We have ships and boats for going under water, and brooking of seas; also swimming-girdles and supporters. We have divers curious clocks, and other like motions of return: and some perpetual motions. We imitate also motions of living creatures, by images, of men, beasts, birds, fishes, and serpents. We have also a great number of other various motions, strange for equality, fineness, and subtilty.

"We have also a mathematical house, where are represented all instruments, as well of geometry as astronomy, exquisitely made.

"We have also houses of deceits of the senses; where we represent all manner of feats of juggling, false apparitions, impostures, and illusions; and their fallacies. And surely you will easily believe that we that have so many things truly natural which induce admiration, could in a world of particulars deceive the senses, if we would disguise those things and labour to make them seem more miraculous. But we do hate all impostures, and lies; insomuch as we have severely forbidden it to all our fellows, under pain of ignominy and fines, that they do not show any natural work or thing, adorned or swelling; but only pure as it is, and without all affectation of strangeness.

"These are (my son) the riches of Salomon's House.

"For the several employments and offices of our fellows; we have twelve that sail into foreign countries, under the names of other nations, (for our own we conceal); who bring us the books, and abstracts, and patterns of experiments of all other parts. These we call Merchants of Light.

"We have three that collect the experiments which are in all books. These we call Depredators.

"We have three that collect the experiments of all mechanical arts; and also of liberal sciences; and also of practices which are not brought into arts. These we call Mystery-men.

"We have three that try new experiments, such as themselves think good. These we call Pioneers or Miners.

"We have three that draw the experiments of the former four into titles and tables, to give the better light for the drawing of observations and axioms out of them. These we call Compilers.

"We have three that bend themselves, looking into the experiments of their fellows, and cast about how to draw out of them things of use and practise for man's life, and knowledge, as well for works as for plain demonstration of causes, means of natural divinations, and the easy and clear discovery of the virtues and parts of bodies. These we call Dowry-men or Benefactors.

"Then after divers meetings and consults of our whole number, to consider of the former labours and collections, we have three that take care, out of them, to direct new experiments, of a higher light, more penetrating into nature than the former. These we call Lamps.

"We have three others that do execute the experiments so directed, and report them. These we call Inoculators.

"Lastly, we have three that raise the former discoveries by experiments into greater observations, axioms, and aphorisms. These we call Interpreters of Nature.

"We have also, as you must think, novices and apprentices, that the succession of the former employed men do not fail; besides, a great number of servants and attendants, men and women. And this we do also: we have consultations, which of the inventions and experiences which we have discovered shall be published, and which not: and take all an oath of secrecy, for the concealing of those which we think fit to keep secret: though some of those we do reveal sometimes to the state and some not.

"For our ordinances and rites: we have two very long and fair galleries: in one of these we place patterns and samples of all manner of the more rare and excellent inventions in the other we place the statues of all principal inventors. There we have the statue of your Columbus, that discovered the West Indies: also the inventor of ships: your monk that was the inventor of ordnance and of gunpowder: the inventor of music: the inventor of letters: the inventor of printing: the inventor of observations of astronomy: the inventor of works in metal: the inventor of glass: the inventor of silk of the worm: the inventor of wine: the inventor of corn and bread:

the inventor of sugars: and all these, by more certain tradition than you have. Then have we divers inventors of our own, of excellent works; which since you have not seen, it were too long to make descriptions of them; and besides, in the right understanding of those descriptions you might easily err. For upon every invention of value, we erect a statue to the inventor, and give him a liberal and honourable reward. These statues are some of brass; some of marble and touch-stone; some of cedar and other special woods gilt and adorned; some of iron; some of silver; some of gold.

"We have certain hymns and services, which we say daily, of Lord and thanks to God for his marvellous works: and forms of prayers, imploring his aid and blessing for the illumination of our labours, and the turning of them into good and holy uses.

"Lastly, we have circuits or visits of divers principal cities of the kingdom; where, as it cometh to pass, we do publish such new profitable inventions as we think good. And we do also declare natural divinations of diseases, plagues, swarms-of hurtful creatures, scarcity, tempests, earthquakes, great inundations, comets, temperature of the year, and divers other things; and we give counsel thereupon, what the people shall do for the prevention and remedy of them."

And when he had said this, he stood up; and I, as I had been taught, kneeled down, and he laid his right hand upon my head, and said; "God bless thee, my son; and God bless this relation, which I have made. I give thee leave to publish it for the good of other nations; for we here are in God's bosom, a land unknown." And so he left me; having assigned a value of about two thousand ducats, for a bounty to me and my fellows. For they give great largesses where they come upon all occasions.

[The rest was not perfected.]

Printed in the United Kingdom
by Lightning Source UK Ltd.
134680UK00002B/351/A